Aunt Skilly and the Stranger

by KATHLEEN STEVENS   pictures by ROBERT ANDREW PARKER

Ticknor & Fields Books for Young Readers

NEW YORK   1994

Published by Ticknor & Fields Books for Young Readers
A Houghton Mifflin company, 215 Park Avenue South,
New York, New York 10003.

Manufactured in the United States of America

Book design by David Saylor
The text of this book is set in 15 point ITC Esprit Book
The illustrations are watercolor and ink, reproduced in full color

HOR   10   9   8   7   6   5   4   3   2   1

Library of Congress Cataloging-in-Publication Data
Stevens, Kathleen.
Aunt Skilly and the stranger / by Kathleen Stevens;
illustrated by Robert Andrew Parker.   p. cm.
Summary: A thief makes the mistake of trying to steal homemade
quilts from Aunt Skilly and her goose Buckle.
ISBN 0-395-68712-8
[1. Geese—Fiction. 2. Robbers and outlaws—Fiction.
3. Mountain life—Fiction.] I. Parker, Robert Andrew, ill. II. Title.
PZ7.S84454Au 1994
[E]—dc20   93-38235   CIP   AC

To Eileen, Carole, and Barb, with thanks
K. S.

To Claudia, Mimi, Max, Jack, Russell, Reed, and Will
R. A. P.

IN A SMALL CABIN on the side of Which-Way Mountain
lived an old woman named Aunt Skilly. She had a well for
water, a garden patch for vegetables, and a gray goose named
Buckle for a friend.

One bright September afternoon, Aunt Skilly sat on her
doorstep shucking seed corn. She set aside the husks to fill a
new bed-tick for herself. "You'll eat well from this corn,"
Aunt Skilly told Buckle, who was pecking at bugs in the dust.

A stranger in a slouch hat came riding down the trail. "Howdy," said the stranger. "Can you spare a cup of water for a traveler?"

Buckle hissed.

"Why, Buckle," scolded Aunt Skilly. "That's no way to greet a visitor." She filled a tin cup at the well and gave it to the stranger. "Have you come far, mister?"

"From t'other side of the mountain. Plan to be down in the valley by nightfall." The stranger wiped his mouth on his sleeve. "From up on the trail I saw that fine row of quilts hanging over your clothesline. Colors bright as a rainbow after a thunderstorm."

"Took me all winter to piece those quilts," said Aunt Skilly. "Hung them out to air. Tomorrow the peddler comes to buy them."

The stranger took a closer look. "Prettiest patterns I ever did see. And stitches small as the wings of a firefly. I reckon the peddler will pay a high price for them."

"Enough to keep me and Buckle through the winter," said Aunt Skilly. She hung the tin cup back on its hook. "There's nothing fancy for supper, stranger, but you're welcome to sit at my table."

"That would be right nice." The stranger's eyes flickered around the yard. "If I tie my mule to that sourwood tree, will your hound dog come nipping at his heels?"

"No hound dog here," said Aunt Skilly. "Just me and Buckle."

"No hound dog?" said the stranger. "Well now. I'll just wash up and be in directly."

Aunt Skilly set snap beans to simmering and potatoes to frying.
She put a plate of biscuits and a pot of apple butter on the table.

The stranger sauntered into the cabin with the quilts piled in his arms. "Thought I'd help out," he said.

"Much obliged," said Aunt Skilly. She shook out a gunnysack and slid the quilts inside. The stranger watched as she laid the sack of quilts on a chest in the corner.

"*Ho-n-n-n-k*," said Buckle, peering through the doorway.

"Is it time for your supper too, my good gray goose?" Aunt Skilly scattered seed corn in the yard, then turned to the stranger. "Pull up a chair and take your needs."

As the stranger piled his plate, his mule let out a noisy *hee-haw! hee-haw!* The stranger frowned. "My mule brays louder than a buzz saw grinding knots in a hickory log. I reckon your neighbors will be coming round to see what's causing all the racket."

"Not likely," said Aunt Skilly. "Closest neighbor lives a mile away."

"Is that so?" The stranger smiled and helped himself to another biscuit.

When his plate was empty, he pushed back his chair. "Mighty fine supper. You cook as good as you piece quilts. Now I'd best be on my way."

With his hand on the latch, the stranger turned to Aunt Skilly. "I noticed that your door has no bar."

"No need for a bar," said Aunt Skilly. "Only honest folks live on this side of Which-Way Mountain."

The stranger pulled his hat lower. "Then you're luckier than the folks who live on the other side."

Aunt Skilly watched from the doorway as the stranger mounted his mule and swayed down the trail. Then she scrubbed the supper dishes, carried in the corn, and tidied the cabin. When she was finished, she sat on the doorstep and stroked Buckle's feathers. They listened to crickets fiddling in the dusk. Soon a little pointy moon tiptoed up the sky. "Time for bed, Buckle," said Aunt Skilly.

The goose scuttled under the cabin, and Aunt Skilly went inside.

She brushed her hair, put on her nightgown, and climbed into her wooden bed beneath one of her own warm quilts.

Soon the twist of smoke from Aunt Skilly's chimney dwindled to a thread.

Far off in the woods, an owl hooted.

A branch cracked at the edge of the clearing.

A dark figure stepped out from the underbrush and crept toward the cabin.

Softly, the latch lifted.
Softly, the door opened.
Aunt Skilly slept on.

The figure stole toward the chest, picked up the sack,
and turned to leave. . . .
A floorboard creaked.

Aunt Skilly woke with a start. "Who's there?" she called.

Heavy boots clattered across the floor.
"Stop, thief!" cried Aunt Skilly.
But the intruder ran into the yard.

A shadow burst from beneath the cabin. A long neck stretched out and powerful wings beat the air. The gray goose attacked.

The intruder crashed into the woods. Buckle flapped after him, hissing and nipping at his heels.

Aunt Skilly appeared in the doorway, holding a flickering fat-pine stick that lit up the yard. Trampled in the dust lay an old slouch hat. "Why, that rascal! He did come back to steal my quilts!" said Aunt Skilly.

Buckle pattered out of the bushes.

"Good for you, Buckle! You scared him into the next county. Come inside now. You deserve a treat."

Aunt Skilly heaped a bowl with seed corn and set it on the floor. "That stranger was one part muscle and nine parts fool," she said, lifting the lid of the wooden chest. Inside, neatly folded and safe from harm, were her beautiful quilts.

The next morning the peddler's wagon creaked into Aunt Skilly's yard.
"Saw a curious sight on my way up the mountain," said the peddler,
counting out Aunt Skilly's money. "There's a heap of corn shucks scattered
in the middle of the trail, with an empty gunnysack alongside."

"Is that right?" said Aunt Skilly.

The peddler tucked Aunt Skilly's quilts into his wagon. "These fine quilts of yours will warm many a cold body this winter."

"Better than lining the pockets of a thief," chuckled Aunt Skilly. "Isn't that so, Buckle?"

And the gray goose said, *"Ho-n-n-n-k!"*